MILLIE: BOOK FOUR
DANDELION DAYS
TROON HARRISON

**Look for the other Millie stories
in Our Canadian Girl**

MILLIE: BOOK FOUR
DANDELION
DAYS
TROON HARRISON

PENGUIN
CANADA

PENGUIN CANADA

Published by the Penguin Group

Penguin Group (Canada), 90 Eglinton Avenue East, Suite 700, Toronto, Ontario, Canada M4P 2Y
(a division of Pearson Canada Inc.)

Penguin Group (USA) Inc., 375 Hudson Street, New York, New York 10014, U.S.A.
Penguin Books Ltd, 80 Strand, London WC2R 0RL, England
Penguin Ireland, 25 St Stephen's Green, Dublin 2, Ireland (a division of Penguin Books Ltd)
Penguin Group (Australia), 250 Camberwell Road, Camberwell, Victoria 3124, Australia
(a division of Pearson Australia Group Pty Ltd)
Penguin Books India Pvt Ltd, 11 Community Centre, Panchsheel Park, New Delhi – 110 017, Indi
Penguin Group (NZ), 67 Apollo Drive, Rosedale, North Shore 0632, New Zealand
(a division of Pearson New Zealand Ltd)
Penguin Books (South Africa) (Pty) Ltd, 24 Sturdee Avenue, Rosebank, Johannesburg 2196,
South Africa

Penguin Books Ltd, Registered Offices: 80 Strand, London WC2R 0RL, England

First published 2007

1 2 3 4 5 6 7 8 9 10   (WEB)

Copyright © Troon Harrison, 2007
Illustrations copyright © Janet Wilson, 2007
Design: Matthews Communications Design Inc.
Map copyright © Sharon Matthews

*Publisher's note: This book is a work of fiction. Names, characters, places, and incidents
either are the product of the author's imagination or are used fictitiously, and any
resemblance to actual persons living or dead, events, or locales is entirely coincidental.*

Manufactured in Canada.

Library and Archives Canada Cataloguing in Publication data available upon request.

ISBN-13: 978-0-14-305453-5
ISBN-10: 0-14-305453-8

Visit the Penguin Group (Canada) website at **www.penguin.ca**

Special and corporate bulk purchase rates available; please see
www.penguin.ca/corporatesales or call 1-800-399-6858, ext. 477 or 474

For my mother,
extraordinary in her capacity to love
and nurture her children
and grandchildren;
she is our guardian angel

Canada

Quebec

Newfoundland and Labrador

P.E.I.

Nova Scotia

New Brunswick

 Marks the location of the story

MILLIE'S SPRING

You may sometimes grumble about going to school, but imagine a world where, because your family was poor, you had to work on a farm or in a dangerous factory instead! Your working day might be as long as fourteen hours, and you wouldn't be able to quit your job because your wages were needed to help buy food or pay rent. This scenario was real for many children in Ontario in the early twentieth century.

Before 1867, when Canada became a country, children as young as six years old worked. By 1871, children in Ontario under the age of fourteen were required by law to attend school, but many were still kept away from class to work. Then, in 1884, when children made up 11 per cent of the workforce in the city of Toronto—that's more than one worker out of ten—the Factory Act became law in Ontario. This new law stated that young people could not work more than sixty hours a week and not more than ten hours a day (most adult jobs today are forty hours a week, eight hours a day), and that they had to be allowed one hour for lunch. Unfortunately, the law was hard to enforce and was often ignored, and so children continued to work long hours. In 1908, the Child Labour Act of Ontario forbade children under the age of twelve from working in stores and children under fourteen from working in factories.

By 1905, all provinces except Quebec also had laws that provided free schools for children, so that it was easier to choose to send children to school instead of to work. However, family poverty, the large amount of work to be done on farms, and long distances to school meant that many children continued working instead of sitting in class. In 1921, only one out of every four children over the age of fourteen attended high school. This law too was hard to enforce and thus often ignored. In fact, in 1937, Toronto messenger and delivery boys—many as young as twelve—pleaded with the premier over their working conditions, asking not to be put to work more than sixty hours per week.

Women often did the same work as men but were usually paid lower wages. This made it very difficult for widowed women, or women whose husbands were away or in jail, to support their own children. In 1912, the Vancouver Trades and Labour Council's newspaper argued that women's wages needed to be raised as women "could not support themselves on the low wages paid to them by employers." Ontario passed a Minimum Wage Act in 1920, but fewer than half of women workers were even covered. Women's low wages also contributed to children having to work to help support their families.

Millie knows about this problem because of her friend Molly, an immigrant child who lived in the slums of Toronto's "Ward" district. When Molly's mother could no longer care for her children, the family was split up by the Children's Aid Society, which had been formed to help neglected or abused children. Molly was sent to a foster home, but by Christmas she had run away.

In 1915, the suffragist Nellie McClung argued for old age pensions, mother's allowances, and public health nursing with free medical and dental treatment in schools. These measures, she believed, would help alleviate poverty, and thus end child labour. In 1916, the province of Manitoba passed its Mothers' Allowance Act: if a father was absent from a family due to a jail term, death, disability, or insanity, the government would provide funding so that the mother could stay home to raise her children. Saskatchewan, Alberta, British Columbia, and Ontario soon passed similar laws.

Even these didn't cover all needs: Unemployment Insurance was not introduced until 1941, and the Family Allowance, which gave money to all sorts of families with children, was not introduced until 1944.

But in 1915, Molly's mother did not have any such government help, and so she couldn't care for her children. After Christmas, Molly was placed in a second foster home, on a farm in the countryside north of Toronto. In those days, you did not have to travel far up Yonge Street to reach farmland. When Millie arrives at York Mills, now part of the city of Toronto, it is a small village on the banks of the Don River. Millie anticipates a carefree outdoor adventure on the farm, but the reality that meets her is very different. She learns how hard women and children work on farms, and that Molly and she are expected to work just as hard as the others, at a host of household chores. Much of the work that is now done by appliances, such as vacuum cleaners, washers and dryers, sewing machines, and microwave ovens, was still very labour intensive in 1915. As well as working in the house, women on farms took care of poultry, sold eggs, milked cows, churned butter, and planted and tended large vegetable gardens—and then processed the produce.

Millie also discovers that many children working on farms are not even living with their own families. These "home children" were orphans or children from poor families sent to Canada from England by Dr. Thomas Barnardo's and other organizations. Between 1882 and 1939, many thousands of children were sent to work in Canada. And in 1908, nine out of ten of those children were working on farms. It has been estimated that "without the assistance of children, as farm labourers and domestics, progress on the Canadian farm was almost impossible." Many Barnardo children were treated decently by their farm families, but others were abused and neglected; some of them ran away. Millie helps to rescue one runaway from the river after he has been beaten for neglecting his chores. Although children were supposed to attend school, farm children were often kept home to work on the land. Barnardo boys on farms worked from around 5 in the morning until 9 or 10 at night. For children who did go to school, chores had to be done before school, including feeding cattle and pigs, milking cows, and cleaning stables.

Millie realizes that her life is privileged and even luxurious compared to the lives of many of her peers, who work long hours on farms and in factories so that they can help their families survive. She realizes that being at school is not so bad, and that her friendships at school are important.

CHAPTER N.º 1

"What do you mean—lost?" I demanded, stopping under a maple tree to stare at my friend Edwina.

She shrugged. "I didn't know Elsie's brother would lose it," she retorted. "It's not my fault."

"But you should never have loaned him my mouth organ!"

"Maybe it will reappear," Edwina replied, and sauntered on past my house toward her own. The bright sunlight of early May threw her sharp shadow onto the first green grass. A robin flew overhead.

I fumed as I stomped around to the back door and into the kitchen: how could she have done this with my mouth organ, my prize possession? Bertha, our housekeeper and cook, looked up from kneading bread dough.

"What's the matter?" she asked. "You've a face like a wet Monday."

"Edwina isn't my friend any more—she's getting on my nerves," I muttered, taking a cheese scone from the basket on the counter.

"Go on with you." Bertha's hands slapped the dough. "Edwina's been your best friend all school year."

"Not any more." I bit deep into the scone, staring at the floor. My chest felt hot and knotted with anger, but also with a sorrow I didn't want to admit to. It was true: Edwina had been my best friend, at least until around Easter, when she had started playing with another girl from school, Elsie, instead. Elsie had a dog with a red leather collar, and an older brother called William, with whom half the girls in class said they were in love. Elsie played hockey on the university campus rink, and her brother had seen the horses diving off the wooden tower at Hanlan's Point. I was sick of hearing about all the things that Elsie and William did; they were all that Edwina talked about now. I wanted Edwina back for my best friend.

"I'm walking to school by myself from now on," I declared, squinting at the pattern on the floor to stop myself from crying.

"Nonsense," said Bertha. "Your mother won't allow it."

I scraped the chair back and wandered into the parlour. Mother was at the piano bench, leafing through sheet music while my baby sister, Louisa May, crawled on the carpet. Louisa May's mouth curved into a grin when she saw me, showing her new teeth.

"Give your sister a smile," Mother said, then looked over at me. "What's the matter? You're looking very peaky these days, Millie."

I knelt by Louisa May and tickled her chin.

"Nothing," I muttered, but I could feel Mother staring at my bent neck.

"You're still disappointed about not going away at Easter, aren't you?" she asked.

I nodded. "And I miss Father," I said, my lips quivering.

Louisa May chortled happily, but I couldn't smile at her. Sometimes now when I tried to imagine Father's face, I just couldn't. Then panic would flood me: how could I forget my own father's face, with its twinkling blue eyes and mischievous grin? For how much longer would the war in Europe drag on, keeping Father away working as an engineer in England's shipyards? Everyone had said the war would be over by Christmas, but now it was 1915, and the battles still raged.

Mother stroked the back of my head. "We all miss your father," she agreed with a sigh. "Why don't we have a tea party this weekend? You can invite Edwina, and Bertha can bake fairy cakes."

"I don't want Edwina here!" I answered quickly. "She's not my friend any more. Mother, please could I go and visit Molly? Please, Mother?"

I knelt on my heels and stared at Mother as she sighed again and brushed a strand of hair back into her chignon. My friend Molly had been sent to a foster home on a farm after Christmas. At Easter, I had been planning to visit her, but a late storm had blown in from the lake and Mother had changed her mind about my trip.

"She wrote in her letter that she was so disappointed not to see me," I continued. "And she's lonely, Mother. She has no family now, just foster people. And she has to work very hard on the farm."

"Perhaps in the summer holidays," Mother agreed. "Now you need to be in school, even if you are feeling out of sorts."

"Nothing goes right any more!" I cried, and rushed from the room. My feet thudded on the stairs. I flung myself onto the comforting softness of the eiderdown on my bed and pressed my face into it. I did miss Father, and Molly too. And now Edwina was Elsie's best friend and my mouth organ was lost. And Luigi the vegetable seller had moved from our Toronto neighbourhood and taken his beautiful horse, Bella, with him. I missed going to the barn in Luigi's yard and petting Bella. I would tell her about Father, and she would flick her ears back and forth.

After some time, I heard Mother's footsteps on the stairs, and then my bed creaked as she sat beside me. "It's been a long winter," she said. "Perhaps a change of scene would do you good, Millie. Some fresh country air might be what you need."

I sat up and wiped my eyes. "I can go to the farm?"

Mother nodded, then looked stern. "I don't approve of throwing tantrums to get one's way, Millie, so don't make this a habit. You must take your lesson books with you and study in the evenings. And you must help Molly with her chores and not be a nuisance to her foster family."

"Yes!" I agreed—I was so happy that I hardly heard what Mother was saying. Thoughts of green fields and skipping lambs flashed through my mind. Maybe there would be a wooden swing under a tree, or Molly and I could play in the hay mow! Maybe there would be horses!

"I'll talk to Mrs. Simcoe and see what can be arranged," Mother said. "Now come and help bathe Louisa May before dinner."

I slid off the bed. I knew that Mrs. Simcoe worked for the Children's Aid Society and had arranged Molly's foster placement after Molly's father went to jail and her mother could no longer care for the four children.

"Will you talk to her soon?" I asked.

"Patience is a virtue," Mother responded, lifting Louisa May from the carpet. Then she smiled. "I'll talk to her tomorrow."

All the next day at school my mind wandered to Mother's promise, and I squirmed restlessly in

my seat. "Stop fidgeting," my teacher repri-
manded, but still my toes kept tapping the floor-
boards. After dismissal, I skipped home ahead of
Edwina and rushed indoors to find Mother. "Can
I go to the farm?" I asked breathlessly.

Mother paused in the writing she was doing at
her desk. "Yes," she said. "Mrs. Simcoe has tele-
phoned Molly's family, and they're expecting you
for a visit next week. You'll travel by radial to
York Mills with Mrs. Simcoe, and Molly's foster
mother will meet you there with a horse and
buggy."

"Oh thank you!" I cried, flinging my arms
around Mother's neck. This would be an adventure, I thought—just like my trip last summer to
the Kawartha Lakes. I loved to travel out of the
city and spend time outdoors, "running wild" as
Mother called it.

The radial, Mrs. Simcoe explained as we waited for it to arrive at the stop, was really a streetcar. It was powered by electricity and ran along a set of shining tracks, like the ones trains ran on. It even looked like a train, I saw as it slid toward us, with its several carriages linked together and lined with windows. The faces of other passengers peered out as we climbed aboard. With a lurch, the radial began to move again, heading north up Yonge Street toward the edge of the city. Passengers swayed and jolted as the radial gained speed; buildings flashed past. I saw hotels and shops, churches, and houses with apple trees in their gardens. A wooden sidewalk edged the road. Motor cars and horse-pulled wagons struggled through Yonge Street's deep, muddy ruts and splashed across puddles.

"This thing is going to be the death of us," Mrs. Simcoe muttered as the radial gained even more speed, swooping down a long hill. Trees and cedar fences swept past. I grinned with excitement. "Are we almost there?" I asked as the radial approached a stop.

"This is Mount Pleasant," Mrs. Simcoe said. "York Mills is the next place."

We had left the city of Toronto behind us now. I peered out at fields where cattle grazed beneath shady oaks or wandered by small creeks. Tall, swaying pine trees lined the street. Then the radial began to slow again, and looking ahead, I saw another village with a general store and post office, a church, and several horses and buggies waiting by the radial tracks. Just as we pulled into the centre of the village, I heard a shout. The radial's brakes squealed loudly; passengers were jolted off balance, and a parcel flew to the floor.

"What's the matter?" someone cried.

I looked out and saw a scruffy white dog leap from beneath the radial's spinning wheels with a terrified yelp.

"Was it hit?" a passenger asked, but no one seemed to know.

"Wouldn't be the first time this thing's hit a poor animal," another passenger said. "I heard tell it hit a cow only last month."

I craned my neck, trying to see where the dog had disappeared to. Then I saw it, limping into the shadows beneath a porch. "We must see if it's hurt!" I cried, jumping from my seat and down the steps of the tram into the muddy road. I squelched across to the porch and stooped to look underneath. The dog stared back at me. It was a small terrier with a wiry coat, a brown spot around one eye, and another on its back. It whimpered and shivered. "Come out, I won't hurt you," I coaxed it.

"Miss Millie, you're getting muddy," scolded Mrs. Simcoe behind me, "and you're keeping us all waiting. They say the dog is a stray, so leave it alone and come now."

"We can't leave the dog alone here!" I cried. "Its paw is hurt." And I continued to coax the terrier until at last it crawled from under the porch and pressed against my knees. Its tongue darted out and licked my hand.

"Millie!" cried a voice at that moment, and I looked up to see Molly rushing toward me with her black hair flying behind her. I grinned with pleasure as we hugged.

"Wotcher got 'ere?" Molly asked.

"A stray dog," I answered. "I want to keep him."

"No, no!" protested Mrs. Simcoe, but Molly's face split into a huge grin. "Poor scampy beggar," she said. "Bring 'im along wiv you to the farm."

I picked up the terrier, which was still shaking with fright, and followed Molly toward the waiting buggy while Mrs. Simcoe floundered behind us, protesting. The dog licked my chin and I laughed aloud. Maybe I could even take it home to the city at the end of the week, and maybe Mother would let me keep it!

I continued to coax the terrier until at last it crawled from under the porch and pressed against my knees. Its tongue darted out and licked my hand.

Molly's foster mother was called Mrs. Smith; she was a tall, angular woman with black hair, and dressed all in brown, who sat upright in the buggy. "Hello, Millie," she greeted me, smiling. "Is this your dog?"

"It's a stray," I replied, "but I would like to keep it."

Mrs. Smith clucked her tongue and looked at Mrs. Simcoe with raised eyebrows, then she smiled again. "One more mouth to feed at the farm won't make much difference for a week," she said. "Up you get." And she reached out and lifted the dog into the buggy so that I could climb in too. Her hands as she passed the dog back to me were rough and red from work. Molly scrambled in beside me and stroked the dog's head while the two women chatted, then Mrs. Simcoe turned and walked back to the radial stop.

"Get up!" Mrs. Simcoe commanded her black horse. It strained in the harness, and with a lurch and the sucking sound of mud, the buggy began to move. We passed the Don River, a lumber mill where saw blades whined, and a grist mill where farmers brought their wheat for grinding. After some time, we turned onto the fifteenth concession line and travelled between cedar fences, beneath elm trees, and past fields where wheat already sprouted in bright green rows. Our horse began to trot, hooves crunching on stones and mane flying. Cows bawled in the distance and a dog barked; my terrier pricked its ears.

"Wotcher callin' 'im then?" Molly asked.

"Patches," I decided.

Mrs. Simcoe began to whistle as she drove, and I stared in surprise at her straight back in the seat ahead of me, then tried not to giggle. Mother said that whistling women and crowing hens always came to some bad end, but Mrs. Smith looked like she'd be in charge of whatever happened to her.

"Do you like it at the farm?" I asked Molly quietly.

She shrugged her bony shoulders. "S'all right. There's more work than you can shake a stick at—washin' laundry and cookin' meals, carryin' wood, feedin' the animals, diggin' in the garden. Last month we cooked a batch of marmalade. She's only got sons left at 'ome, so she wanted a girl to help wiv the women's work."

I stared at Molly wide-eyed. "Don't you go to school?"

"Some days. Other days I'm needed to work. Spring's busy on the farm—she's a demon for spring cleanin' and now her daughter's comin' 'ome from teachin' school in Newmarket.

She's gettin' married next week, so it's clean, clean and bake, bake. Still, it's better'n workin' in a factory like I'd be doin' in the city."

"You're too young to work in a factory," I said.

Molly flashed me a scornful look. "'Course I'm not! Scores of kids my age work in factories, sewin' clothes and buildin' stuff. Twelve hours a day. Gettin' fingers chopped off in the machines. Not everyone's like you rich nobs, just sittin' in school all day."

I was silent, stroking Patches's ears. The only work I ever did at home was making cookies with Mother—which was really more for fun—or practising the piano. Bertha did the house-cleaning and cooked our meals. Maybe my week at the farm was not going to be the adventure I'd imagined.

"Cheer up," Molly said, digging her elbow into me. "We can give 'er the slip and play outside. And 'ere we are—the gates of Rome."

The horse swung into a long driveway lined with maples; at the end stood a square, white-boarded house with gingerbread trim under its eaves. A screened porch ran along the front of the house; to one side, I saw the black soil of a freshly dug vegetable garden. Hens scattered, clucking, at the horse's feet, and a huge golden work horse neighed in the pasture beside the log barn.

"Out you jump and put the kettle on," Mrs. Smith said.

Patches squirmed in my arms when a shaggy dog rushed forward, barking. "Shut yer yap!" Molly commanded the dog, and it turned and ran after the buggy as Mrs. Smith drove away to unhitch the black horse.

"Bring Patches inside—we can look at 'is paw," Molly said, and I followed her up the steps, across the porch, and into the large kitchen. Molly took a kettle out to the pump in the yard. I heard the squeaking as she worked the long handle and water gushed out. She set the kettle with a clang onto the black top of the wood stove and then lifted the lid of a pot and sniffed loudly. "Mutton stew," she said. "Least they feed yer well 'ere. Put Patches down on that blanket by the stove—we use it fer sick young things."

Patches looked happy to be lying by the stove's warmth, and then even happier when Molly sneaked him some mutton stew and gave it to him in a bowl. "Mum's the word," she whispered to me, smiling cheekily and laying her finger across her lips. We looked at Patches's paw while he licked his dish clean. The paw had a cut across the bottom. We decided to wash it and bandage it with strips of cotton torn from an old dress that Molly found in the rag bag. Patches went to sleep after this, snoring. I thought there was a twinkle in his eyes before he closed them.

"Now, let's Botany Bay before we 'ave to start workin'," Molly said. "You know—run for it." She started toward the door, but we were too late. Mrs. Smith was climbing the steps outside.

"There you are then," she said. "Now that your friend is here, Molly, you'll have help with your chores. I want to clean the parlour this afternoon.

We'll take everything out. The men will lift the furniture."

Molly groaned, but Mrs. Smith ignored her and sent her to fetch water to heat on the stove. "And Millie," she said to me, "we'll need more wood."

She gestured to the box beside the stove, and I saw that it was empty save for splinters and bark chips. "The woodpile is beside the porch."

I nodded and skipped out into the sunshine, then staggered back in with several armloads of wood. Molly opened the firebox door and shoved wood inside; flames roared and licked around the pieces. When the water was warm, Mrs. Smith carried it into the parlour, where two young men were moving furniture out into the hallway. Mrs. Smith nodded at them. "Thank you, Nathan and James."

" 'Er Bath buns," Molly whispered.

As usual, I wasn't sure what Molly was talking about, but I guessed by their angular frames and black hair that Nathan and James were

Mrs. Smith's sons. They strode away in their stocking feet and pulled their boots on by the door, heading off to work in the fields again.

"Now then," Mrs Smith said. "We'll carry the carpets outside and beat them. Molly, you can help with that. Millie, you use this water to wash the floor."

I nodded. Once Molly had carried the carpets away, I knelt and began to clean the floor with a rag and the gritty homemade soap that Mrs. Smith gave me. To and fro, to and fro I rubbed the rag across the floor, then rinsed it in the pail of water, wrung it out, and washed another patch of floor. My back ached and my knees hurt from the hard boards. The floor seemed huge. Once I stood up and went to the window. Pulling aside the lace netting, I saw Molly standing at the clothesline, beating the carpets that were hung over it. Dust puffed into the air each time she whacked a carpet. I sighed and bent my knees again.

Finally Mrs. Smith strode in, surveyed my clean floor, and praised my work. I thought that maybe now I'd be able to go outside and explore, but she placed her red hands on her hips and said, "We'll take down the drapes and wash them, then all that furniture in the hall must be dusted before the boys carry it back in."

I sighed and nodded. While I cleaned the table, the piano, and the backs of the wooden chairs standing in the hall, Mrs. Smith fetched a stool and climbed up on it to unfasten the curtain hooks, then carried the curtains into the kitchen. Glancing down that way, I could see her bent over a washtub of steaming water and rubbing the fabric up and down against a washboard. After a while, she wrung the fabric in her strong hands and carried it outside to hang over the line. I rubbed and polished the wooden chairs until my arms ached. The smell of mutton stew made my stomach rumble, and I wondered what time it was. Surely this long afternoon would soon be over.

"Millie!" Mrs. Smith called from the kitchen. "Leave that now and chop this rhubarb for dessert. I do believe the pie is all gone."

I stumbled down the hallway and began to chop the long, red stems of fresh rhubarb that Mrs. Smith had laid on the table. The stems crunched beneath the knife. When I popped a piece into my mouth, the sourness puckered my lips.

"Can you make pastry?" Mrs Smith asked. I shook my head.

"Mercy me!" she replied, sounding surprised. "My Amelia could make the flakiest pastry by the time she was your age. Well, I shall have to finish the pies myself. You run out and fetch the hens in; Molly will show you to where. And ask her to bring in the cows."

I pulled my muddy boots on and clumped down the front steps to look for Molly. I had never felt so tired in my life, but at least now I was outside and not stuck cleaning furniture—I hated housework! When I grew up, I vowed, I would never care about polishing chair backs. What difference did it make anyway? They looked just the same after I'd polished them as they had before!

"Millie!" I saw Molly waving from beside a small wooden shed. The hens were running to her on their yellow legs. "We gotta put 'em away for the night," Molly explained. "Then let 'em out in the morning. Feed 'em. Collect the eggs. The men look after the fields and the horses, but the womenfolk look after the hens and the dairy."

I peered past her to see the hens flapping up into wooden boxes filled with straw where they nestled and clucked sleepily. Molly closed the door on its sagging leather hinges and slid a wooden bar across. "Keep out the boogie man," she said, winking.

"Mrs Smith says—"

"Bring in the cows," Molly interrupted. "Cripes, I know what to bloomin' do—I been bringin' 'em in all month. Come on."

We tramped across the pasture with the big dog, Major, running around us. In the distance, in the evening sunshine, the herd of cattle grazed on the lush grass. Molly tipped her head back and called, and Major ran around the cows barking. Slowly they drifted toward us.

"Are they safe?" I whispered. I had never been close to a cow before.

"Safe as 'ouses," Molly said. "'Less they kick you."

I watched the cows nervously, unsure whether Molly was joking. Their tails swung at flies. Their cleft hooves slipped on the damp ground. Their bare noses were smooth-looking, and their brown eyes calm and gentle. I stared in fascination at their black and white coats and their curled horns. "Holsteins," Molly said.

The cows followed each other into the shadows of the barn and stood quietly in their stalls while Molly showed me how to feed them hay. Soon Mrs. Smith, her sons, and a tall, bearded man who was Mr. Smith joined us and pulled out wooden stools. I watched as they sat beside the cows and began to milk them into metal buckets; the milk squirted with rhythmic whooshing sounds. Striped barn cats twined around the legs of the stools, meowing. "Want to try?" Molly asked. She placed a stool beside a cow and patted the seat. "Come on," she coaxed. "Thought you liked animals. This 'ere cow's called Annabelle."

I sat on the stool; the smell of Annabelle filled my nose, and I saw her sides moving in and out with her breath. "Give 'er a good squeeze," Molly instructed. I grasped a teat in my hand; it felt warm and firm. I squeezed and squeezed but no milk came out. Finally Molly snorted and nudged me off the stool. "You gotta squeeze and pull at the same time," she said, showing me how. A thin stream of milk pinged against the pail. I tried again, and this time I managed to make the milk hit the pail too. I kept squeezing and pulling. The milk hissed, covering the bottom of the pail. Surely it must be getting full by now. I checked and saw only an inch of frothy milk in my pail. I groaned. My arms and hands burned with cramps. How did the Smiths fill whole pails with milk?

"I'll finish this," Mrs. Smith said. "You girls go up to the house and set the table and take those pies out of the oven."

Together, Molly and I crossed the yard, too tired to talk. We took turns pumping the handle and washing our hands; the freezing water numbed my fingers. Inside the kitchen, Molly lit a lamp and Patches blinked sleepily on his blanket. Then Molly sliced up a whole loaf of bread while I took the rhubarb pies from the oven. Heat shimmered against my face, and I flinched, and when my hand brushed the oven wall, I felt a searing pain. I almost dropped the pie. Hastily I set it on the table and pressed my hand to my mouth.

"Burn yerself?" Molly asked. "She makes some salve fer that." She reached up for a small pot on a shelf by the stove, unscrewed the lid, and smeared ointment onto my hand.

The family clomped up the steps and pulled their boots off, then entered to sit around the large wooden table. "After supper, that

I squeezed and squeezed
but no milk came out.

furniture can be put back in the parlour," Mrs Smith said.

"Aw—this evening?" James complained, and his father shot him a stern look.

"You heard your mother," he said, and James bent over his stew.

While James and Nathan moved the furniture, Mr. Smith returned to the barn to check on a cow that he said was going to have a calf very soon. Mrs. Smith sat under the lamp hemming a sheet for her daughter's new home. Her needle flashed in and out of the white cotton, and she talked about her daughter Amelia's wedding just as fast as she sewed.

"I must make the almond paste for the cake," she said. "And end of this week we'll kill and pluck hens. There are enough apples left in the barrels from last summer that we can make a good number of pies. And I'll buy oysters for stuffing the fowl. And we'll have boiled hams, too. What a mercy the hogs did so well last year—there's still plenty of meat in the smokehouse."

It sounded to me like a whole passel of work, and Molly must have thought so too because she rolled her eyes at me.

"You girls work hard and learn to be good cooks and housewives. Then maybe you'll be fortunate enough to find yourselves husbands as good as my Amelia's Gordon."

Molly rolled her eyes again. "Like gettin' cut and carried solved me ma's problems," she muttered.

While Mrs. Smith talked and sewed, Molly and I washed the dishes, refilled the wood box, carried water from the pump, and swept the kitchen floor with a broom. When it was finally time for bed, I was so tired I could hardly climb the creaking stairs.

I lay beside Molly, aching all over. "Is it like this every day?" I asked her.

"Pretty much," Molly said, yawning.

I stared into the darkness. Animals howled in the distance and the hair rose on the back of my neck. "What is that?" I whispered.

"Coyotes," Molly mumbled. Soon her breath-ing grew slow and even; she was asleep. But I lay rigid, wondering if I'd made a big mistake. Even though I knew that the radial ran along Yonge Street every day, I felt such a long way from home that my stomach hurt.

CHAPTER N° 3

On my second day at the farm, Molly and I were awakened by Mrs. Smith shouting up the stairs. Molly groaned and pulled a pillow over her head. Our room was so dark that even the white wash jug and bowl on the bureau were invisible. Was it the middle of the night? Why were we being called? "Bloomin' work to do, ain't it?" Molly grumbled.

We tumbled from bed into the chilly air and hastily pulled on socks and flannel petticoats. When we reached the kitchen, we found the wood stove already lit and sending out a pleasant warmth, but there was no time to warm our fingers. "I'll need help churning butter this morning," Mrs. Smith said. "Molly, you can do that while Millie fetches the eggs. Then I'm taking our milk to the cheese factory. Eat up quick and get those pans washed."

I squinted sleepily at the table where porridge steamed in bowls. The three men came in from the barn, smelling of cows and horses, and sat down and shovelled food into their mouths without speaking much.

"Need to harrow the top twenty and get the rye in," Mr. Smith finally said. "James, you harness the team right after milking. And Nathan, you take the broken plowshare into York Mills and get the smith to repair it."

As soon as their bowls were empty, the men headed out into the dawn light to milk the cows. Molly and I washed the dishes in water that had been heated on the stove, then sat on the front porch and took seeds out of a bowlful of raisins— Mrs. Smith wanted to bake raisin buns for Amelia's wedding. While Mrs. Smith drove the milk cans to the cheese factory, Molly and I collected eggs, let the hens out, and cleaned their coop. The eggs were a lovely surprise, lying warm and smooth in the nests, but cleaning the coop was a messy, stinky job that made my eyes water. I shot longing glances toward the pastures, but the black horse was away to the cheese factory, and the big horses were pulling a harrow in the top fields. I wished I could escape from chores and make friends with a horse, like I had done with Bella.

Once the coop was clean, I ran in to find Patches. His tail wagged when he saw me, and his lips grinned when I hugged his bony ribs. "You're *my* dog now," I promised him. Surely Mother would let me keep him—surely even she would love his twinkling dark eyes and the way his tongue licked my chin. I changed the bandage on his foot, and then heard Mrs. Smith returning at a fast trot.

All that day and the day that followed, Molly and I worked, mostly in the house. We pulled the feather ticks from the beds and changed them for the straw summer ticks. We washed walls and woodwork, and polished picture frames, and slapped the dust from cushions. We starched and ironed shirts and petticoats and sheets, the wood stove's heat beating at our backs as it warmed the irons. We dug the garden over, watching robins hop after worms, and planted lettuce and radish. In the pantry, we lifted down bottles of relish and pickles and canned tomatoes, beans, and corn preserved from last summer's garden. There were homemade jams too—strawberry-rhubarb, red currant, gooseberry. We wiped the jars clean and the shelves beneath. We spent a messy afternoon, with the help of the men, taking down the stovepipes and cleaning them. Everyone hated the greasy black soot; our hands and faces were smeared in it. The men were anxious to get away to the fields—Mr. Smith kept looking at the clear sky and muttering about the possibility of the weather changing. We baked bread, kneading the dough until my shoulders cramped and I wanted to scream. Three times daily, we served meals for the men who came in from the fields dirty, wind burned, and tired. They ate mountains of food.

Finally, in mid-afternoon on the third day, I couldn't take it any more. Through the window, I could see Patches trotting in the yard, using all four legs. If only he and I could run through the pastures! This was not a holiday that I was having with Molly—we were working like slaves. I flung down the potato I was peeling and let my knife go with a clatter.

"Wot's up?" Molly asked.

"I'm going outside to explore," I said. "I'm going to go see the black horse."

Molly gaped at me, then her devilish grin split her thin cheeks and she flung down her own potato and peeler and jumped ahead of me out the door.

"Here, Patches!" I yelled, and he ran across the yard to my heels as Molly and I raced to the pasture behind the log barn. Molly disappeared inside briefly and returned with a bridle on her shoulder. "Now you can ride 'im," she said, "like you rode Bella."

"My cousin was with me then," I pointed out. "I can't ride on my own."

"'Course you can," Molly retorted. "You rode Bella all the way to Ashbridges Marshes, so what d'yer mean, yer can't ride?" Her dark, street-smart eyes challenged me fiercely. I remembered how good it had felt to ride along Queen Street on beautiful Bella, with her nodding neck and flicking ears.

"Well, maybe I can ride a little," I said.

Molly climbed over the fence of split white cedar and I followed while Patches crawled beneath the bottom rail. "Prince! Prince!" Molly called. The black horse drifted across the grass, watching us curiously. He seemed huge up close; his glossy shoulders were level with my head, and breath snorted from his velvety nostrils. I kept my toes well away from his huge hooves. But, I thought, looking at his arched neck and large eyes, he was beautiful. Molly held out a carrot and Prince bent his head to eat; she slipped the bit into his mouth and the bridle over his ears. Then she led him alongside the fence.

"Up yer get!" she told me.

I stared at the horse's high back. "I don't think I can ride," I said, but Molly only laughed. "You rode Bella, so now ride Prince!" she insisted.

I climbed up on the fence, waving my arms for balance, and clutched a handful of mane. Then, with a deep breath, I gathered my courage and slid onto Prince's broad back. Molly led him along and delight swept through me: Prince was as warm and wonderful as Bella had been.

Suddenly we heard Mrs. Smith calling from the house. "I'll go back—you ride," Molly said, letting go of the reins.

"Wait—don't leave me!" I cried, but Molly was already over the fence and running toward the house. "Coming, Mrs Smith!" I heard her faint cry.

I stared down at the ground; it seemed very far below me. Prince walked along calmly, though, and after a few minutes my heart stopped pounding. I pulled the reins and Prince turned so that we rode behind a patch of maple that hid us from the farmhouse. Beneath the trees the ground was white with trillium flowers. We crossed the next pasture, with Patches following, and went down a sloping field scattered with willows to where a river wound through the land. Mrs. Smith had said that the Don River flowed through a corner of the farm, and so I thought this must be it.

Prince slipped down the bank and lowered his head for a drink; water gurgled from his mouth. I leaned over his neck and laid my face on his shining mane. Having a horse would be even better, I thought, than having a dog. But I would never be able to keep a horse in the city. "You have to make Mother love you," I warned Patches as he lapped water beside Prince. Suddenly Patches barked and Prince lifted his head, with his ears pricked. I heard a cry and looked up.

Around a bend in the river came a thrashing shape: a large stick? a stump? an animal? I saw a dark head, then flailing arms. As the person swept closer, I realized I was seeing a boy only a little older than myself; his eyes were filled with water and the dark hole of his mouth opened and closed, hollering for help.

I gripped a handful of mane and dug my heels into Prince's sides. He snorted and sidled along the bank, refusing to enter the water. "Come on!" I yelled. "Get up, Prince!" I hammered my heels against his ribs, and at last, as the boy sank again and swept past, Prince began to wade slowly into the river. I kept shouting at him to hurry, and kicking him, and then suddenly I felt the water lift his great weight free from the muddy bottom, felt the current push him sideways and sweep us along after the drowning boy. Water, still cold from winter, gurgled and dragged at my soaking skirts, and sent chills through me. I pulled on the reins, turning Prince's head toward the boy. The horse struck out strongly with his long legs, pulling us through the water with sure strokes. Breath whistled in and out of his flared nostrils.

"Come on, Prince. You can do it!" I encouraged him, but fear gripped my throat. What if he couldn't reach the boy in time? What if he got tired and couldn't even get himself and me back to shore? We would all drown. I wound his mane tighter around my fingers as the river pulled at my legs. Prince struggled on, raising his head above the water, snorting as it splashed up his nose.

Now we had almost reached the boy, and I saw fear shining in his eyes. "Grab a-hold of his mane!" I shouted over the rush of the water. I reined Prince closer to the boy. A scrawny arm shot from the water and a hand grabbed my leg. The boy's nails cut into my skin through bunches of wet fabric. I slid helplessly across Prince's slippery back, the water rushing up to meet my face.

"Let go of me!" I screamed, slapping at the boy's white knuckles. "Grab the horse! Let go!"

Prince snorted and churned in the water, his eyes rolling white. I kicked out at the boy and tried desperately to cling to Prince. Fear knifed through me—now for sure we were going to drown in the Don's rushing green waters. I was slipping, slipping …

"LET GO!" I screamed again, my throat hurting.

Suddenly the boy reached up with his other arm and caught Prince's mane; I felt his hold release on my leg and managed to pull myself back astride Prince. I dragged on a rein and turned the horse's head for shore. The boy floated, his ripped shirt and ragged pants billowing alongside us in the water as Prince towed him.

On the bank, Patches ran up and down barking. Prince scrambled out and stood heaving, his head down and water streaming from his legs. The boy stretched on the shore, gasping. After a few minutes, he rolled onto one side and retched weakly, coughed and gagged, then breathed more

Prince scrambled out and stood heaving, his head down and water streaming from his legs. The boy stretched on the shore, gasping.

steadily. I watched fearfully from Prince's back. Patches whined uneasily.

"Why did you go into the river if you can't swim?" I asked the boy.

He stared suspiciously at me from under thick, dark eyebrows. His thin face was white as stone and so were his shoulders, although one was marked by a plum-coloured bruise where his shirt was torn.

"Mind your own business," he answered.

"I rescued you!" I protested. "You don't have to be so unfriendly."

The boy glared at the grass and shrugged. "How d'you know I can't swim?"

"You were drowning. How come?"

"Jeez, is that all you do—ask questions?" he said, with an exasperated sigh. "So I fell off my log. Satisfied?"

"Where do you live?"

He gestured with his head, his wet hair falling into his eyes. "'Cross the other side. On a farm."

"How will you get home?" I asked as Prince began to graze.

The boy was silent for some time. "How—" I began again.

"Not going home. Don't have one. That farm ain't my home. It's just a place where I work till I drop. Not that they care. See this?" He wrenched his shirt open and turned so that I could see his back, striped with angry red welts.

"What happened?" I asked.

"Beat me with a belt 'cause I forgot to let the hogs out this morning. And last week, gave me no supper for three nights 'cause I busted a milking stool by accident."

"Your parents did that?" I asked incredulously; I could hardly believe my ears. No wonder the boy's face looked so white below his black hair.

"Not my parents," the boy said scornfully. "They're both dead. Some codger called Doctor Barnardo rounded up a bunch of kids off the streets in England and sent us to Canadian farm families."

"To be adopted?"

"Nah, just to work. Work, work, work."

"But how old are you?" I asked in dismay.

"Thirteen," the boy replied. "Runty ain't I? That's what *they* always say: 'Hey, runt, betcha can't work like a man. Hey, runt, you're too small to need much feeding.'"

"But this is terrible!" I cried as Patches licked the boy's trembling hands. "If I was you, I'd run away."

"Slow, aren't you. Whatcha think I was doin' crossin' the Don on a log?"

"You'd better get on Prince," I decided, "and come back to my farm and have some food."

"Not going to any farm near here and get sent back. I'll hide in your barn and you can bring me grub, then I gotta travel on."

"Promise you'll stay while I try and find you help!" I begged.

The boy stood up; shivers shook his thin body. "Maybe I will, maybe I won't," he said, his teeth chattering. I whistled for Patches and rode Prince alongside a rock where the boy could climb on behind me.

"What's your name?" I asked him as Prince carried us through the pasture back toward the maple woods.

"Think me mom used to call me Mathew, but then on the street they called me Tatters and now all I get is Runt. Even the farm animals got better names."

"Well, I'll call you Mathew," I said firmly. "And if you stay hidden, I can find help for you. My friend Molly is working on this farm, and she never gets beaten. And I know a lady who can find you a better home."

Mathew coughed and shook, and I began shivering too as the breeze tugged at my soaked clothes. I reined Prince in at the edge of the maple woods and stared toward the house.

"You run over to the driving shed," I said, "and hide in the loft; it only has old harness and junk in it. I'll bring you some food."

"I ain't staying 'less you promise not to tell on me."

"I'll only tell Molly, and Mrs. Simcoe who works for Children's Aid," I promised.

Mathew nodded, slid from Prince, and ran to the driving shed. I waited until he slipped through the door, then I let out a sigh of relief. I was going to turn Prince loose, but then I looked at how wet he was. What if he got sick from being cold? What did you do with a wet horse? Could I sneak him into the barn? I glanced all around; the men were still out working, and Mrs. Smith must be in the house, I thought.

"Come on, boy." I led Prince into the barn and began to rub him with straw while Patches snuffled in corners.

"Feel better now?" I said quietly.

"Whatever has happened to you?"

I whirled around, and there was Mrs. Smith in the doorway, her hands on her hips. She didn't look angry, just surprised. "You're wet to the skin! And the horse too?" She stepped closer, peering at Prince.

"We—I—went riding. The long grass must have made his legs wet ..."

Mrs. Smith narrowed her eyes. "Don't you fool with me, Miss Millie. What's been going on?"

"We went swimming in the Don," I stammered, staring at the soaked toes of my boots.

"Swimming? Are you out of your senses, child? Swimming by yourself? And the horse in the water too? I never heard such a crazy notion. I've a good mind to send you packing off home this very day. That dog can stay and catch rats."

"No, please!" I cried. "Mrs. Smith, I won't cause any more trouble!"

If I was sent home, what would happen to Mathew, hidden in the loft of the driving shed? And Mrs. Smith couldn't keep Patches, could she? He was my dog now!

CHAPTER *N° 4*

All the rest of the afternoon, Mrs. Smith kept me where she could see me. First she made me haul and heat water so I could take a bath in a tin tub by the wood stove. "Get that smelly old river off you," she said. Then she told me to sit on the bench under the kitchen window and wrap yarn into balls for Amelia's new home. After this, there was rhubarb to chop for more pies, and dough to stir for buns, and cloth patches to sew onto torn pants. I fidgeted on the bench. I hated sewing! However, I tried to make my stitches as neat as I could in hopes that

Mrs. Smith wouldn't send me home before I'd had time to do something about Mathew. All afternoon, while I worked in the kitchen, I could hear Molly in the basement, sorting through last year's turnips, carrots, and potatoes. Any that were rotting were fed to the hogs, squealing in their pen behind the barn.

Mathew will think I've forgotten him, I thought. What if he doesn't wait but runs away again?

Finally the long afternoon drifted to an end, and Mrs. Smith sent Molly and me out to bring the cows in and lock the chickens up. Finally I had a chance to tell Molly about Mathew. "You must try and save some food," I said. "Then I'll sneak it to him."

"Cripes, Millie, yer gotta nose for trouble like a hound gotta nose for rabbits! Wouldn't it be easier jus' to tell Mrs. Smith? She ain't mean even though she's strict."

"Don't tell!" I hissed. "I promised him!"

"Okay!" she answered. "Don't get yer knickers twisted!"

We shooed the last hen inside and slid the bar across the door, then followed the dogs across the pasture to fetch the cows, which were already wending their way to the barn with flies hovering over them. In the distance, James was driving the team of Belgian horses in from the fields. Milking seemed to take forever, and then Mrs. Smith set Molly and me to scrubbing the dairy floor and cleaning out the butter churn. All the while, I fretted about Mathew, cold and hungry in the driving shed loft. Prince and I were dry, but Mathew was still in wet clothes— if he got sick, it would be my fault.

When we were preparing supper, Molly and I took turns sneaking into the pantry and wrapping food in a cloth. When we heard Mrs. Smith coming, we shoved the bundle behind the flour barrel and rushed back to our jobs. Mrs. Smith gave us a sharp look, and I hung my head over the pot of potatoes I was mashing. I hoped she would think it was the steam making my cheeks burn.

I had planned to sneak out to the barn after we'd eaten, but Mr. Smith said he felt like a tune, and he lifted a fiddle from a case. I groaned inside. I would never get out to the driving shed at this rate! I hopped from foot to foot while Mr. Smith tightened up his bow. The instrument wailed like a cat in a back alley.

"Sit down, Millie," said Mrs. Smith. "You suffer from nerves?"

"I'm fine," I said, and slumped in a chair, trying not to keep gazing out the window and across the yard. The long spring evening had drawn to a close, and now it was fully dark. Stars twinkled and coyotes yowled far off. We sang three hymns and two ballads, and listened to Mr. Smith play a couple of jigs. All I could think of was Mathew crouched shivering in the dark shed, alone and homeless. How scary it must be!

At long last we were sent to bed. I lay in my clothes and waited for the house to settle into silence. Voices muttered. Doors opened and closed. Candle flames were extinguished. Then silence. I tiptoed across the room and down the stairs, gripping the handrail. The stairwell was pitch black and the wooden boards made sounds as loud as gunshots beneath my toes. I sucked in my breath and waited to see if anyone was coming after me. There was no one. I could hear someone snoring.

In the pantry, I felt around for the cloth bundle, then opened the porch door with a terrible squeak. Again I held my breath and waited to see if anyone had heard. Finally, I slipped out onto the steps, where Major and Patches rose to meet me. I pressed my hands into their warm coats with relief, and stood waiting to hear whether the coyotes were howling and how far away they sounded, but the night was silent. I sat down to pull on my boots.

The yard seemed huge, and I could barely see the driving shed. It was never this dark in the city. I ran across the grass, dodging lilac and mock orange bushes. The dogs ran alongside. By touch, I found the driving shed door, its wood splintery and worn, and opened it.

"Mathew?" I called softly. "It's Millie. Are you here?"

There was a rustling overhead, and then he said, "Thought you weren't never going to come. What took so long?"

I heard the scrape of feet on ladder rungs, and then Mathew's breathing as he approached me. As my eyes adjusted, I saw the pale oval of his face beneath an old blanket he'd wrapped around himself like a shawl.

"It was in the cutter," he said. "My clothes'll have to get dried tomorrow. Got any food?"

I handed him the bundle, and we sat down side by side on a wagon while he stuffed bread, pickles, and cold scalloped potatoes into his mouth.

"Did the man—the doctor man—send many children to Canada?" I asked.

"Hundreds, I should think. We come over on a huge ship 'cross the ocean, most water I ever seen. We had to wear tags around our neck. Then they put us on trains and sent us to Toronto, and then I got sent here. They said Canada was a land of opportunity and if we worked hard we'd do well. Huh. I been working like a navvy for two years, and all I got to show for it is beatings. We're free labour, see?"

I was silent. It was hard to imagine that all around us in the peaceful countryside, children were living far from their birthplace and without any family—that they were working so hard on the land. I remembered what Molly had said about poor children working in factories: the long hours, the dangerous machines that caused injuries. I thought of my comfortable city home, my days in school copying work from the board and playing games outside. Suddenly my disagreements with Edwina seemed childish.

"Mathew, I really want to help," I said, "but you must stay hidden until I can talk to Mrs. Simcoe. She's coming to York Mills on Friday to take me home. She'll know what to do."

I felt his shoulders shrug under the blanket, which smelled of horse sweat. "You better keep feeding me," he said.

"I will. And I'll try to find some warmer clothes for you."

He shrugged again. "S'not so cold now spring's come. In winter, I was sleeping in a room next to the woodshed … you never felt such cold."

"No," I mumbled. He was right. I didn't know what it was like to be poor, or cold and hungry, the way that many children did.

"Maybe you'd be warmer hiding in the hayloft," I said, "over the barn. You could run across there now that everyone's in bed. But you'll have to keep hidden in the morning when the cows are milked."

"Reckon that would be a softer bed than the boards of this old shed," Mathew agreed. We swung the door open and peeked out, but the farmhouse was still dark. We scampered across the lawn and the muddy barnyard and into the barn's warm stillness. Suddenly I clutched Mathew's arm. "What's that?"

We stood listening to the whoosh of heavy breathing and to muffled moans. The hair stood up on the nape of my neck. "Mathew?" I whispered.

"Where's the lantern kept?" he hissed.

I fumbled for where it hung on a nail in the doorframe, and handed it by the handle to Mathew, then felt around for matches. The box lay on a shelf; I accidentally knocked it to the floor and stooped to scrabble around for it in the straw, praying not to touch any sloppy cow manure. The whole time I was searching for the matches, the strange noises continued in the dark cavern of the barn, and goosebumps prickled my arms. *Whoosh. Snort. Whoosh. Moan. Whoosh.*

Panic surged in me, then I found the matches and struck one, holding it to the lantern's wick. "Put that match outside in the mud where it can't start a fire," Mathew commanded. I threw the match out, then turned to face the interior of the barn. I felt a little braver now that the lantern's flame made a soft glow. Mathew held it aloft, and huge shadows surged over the wooden walls and the partitions between the stalls. Mathew crept down the aisle. I tiptoed behind him holding my breath.

"Will you look at this!" he said, and I crowded at his side. In a stall lay a golden work horse. The lantern light shone purple in its eyes, and silver in its shaggy mane and tail. Its great hooves lay in the straw, pale as seashells, and its massive stomach rippled and surged with muscles.

"She's foaling," Mathew whispered in awe.

"Does she need help?"

"Dunno."

Mathew hung the lantern on a nail and we slipped into the stall and hunkered down to watch; the mare paid us no attention. For what seemed like hours we crouched, motionless and hardly daring to breathe, while the mare breathed heavily and grunted. She was as huge as I thought a whale would be, or an elephant.

I shuffled closer to her head and ran my hand over her smooth face. "Good girl," I crooned. "You can do it." But inside, I was afraid.

"I think we should get help," I whispered at last.

"Ssh, look."

From between the mare's hind legs appeared a nose covered in white membrane. "The foal's coming!" Mathew said. I gripped his arm with excitement. With a final heave, the mare pushed her baby out into the straw, where it thrashed inside the broken membrane. Its tiny, elegant face appeared, with perfect ears and huge eyes. It struggled to its feet, and so did the mare; she towered over us. Mathew and I shrank against the wall of the stall. The mare licked her foal's curly wet coat, and the foal struggled to stand, swaying on its long legs. It was the most wonderful thing I'd ever seen. Right then and there, I decided I wanted to be an animal doctor and work in barns.

The foal nudged its mother, searching for milk. "What—" I began, and then Mathew and I froze as the barn door swung open and heavy footsteps approached.

"What in tarnation?" Mr. Smith thundered as he came closer. Mathew leapt out of the stall and sprinted away, his feet thudding. "Hey—hey you! Stop right there!" yelled Mr. Smith, making a lunge for Mathew, but Mathew dodged and flashed past him. In a moment, he was out the door, with Patches racing at his heels, barking. The mare snorted and flung up her head; the foal staggered on its new legs and fell into the straw.

"Oh!" I cried.

Mr. Smith came into the stall and knelt down, watching the foal struggle back to its feet.

"Will you look at that!" he marvelled. "A perfect filly—her mother's first. I didn't think she was going to drop her foal so soon. Then I woke and saw the light in the barn." He tore his eyes away from the foal and glared sternly at me.

"What are you doing out here this time of the night? You could have burned the barn down! And who was that boy? I'll not have tramps and strangers on my land."

"He's—Mathew is his name—he's not a tramp," I stammered. "I can't tell you any more, Mr. Smith."

He grabbed my arm and dragged me down the aisle to the barn door, then gave me a shake. "Nonsense!" he roared. "You speak up and tell the truth."

My loyalty to Mathew struggled with my fear; after a moment my words tumbled out. "He's a poor orphan boy, sent from England to work on a farm. But they beat him and he's running away and hiding here. He was drowning in the Don when Prince saved him."

Mr. Smith's face relaxed. "My wife said something about you coming home soaked. A Dr. Barnardo boy, eh? I heard tell they had a boy on the McPherson farm on the sixteenth concession east of the river."

"But you mustn't send him back—please, please!" I cried.

"Lad has to go somewhere; can't live like a vagabond," Mr. Smith said. "Now, I've got to attend to my mare, and you, Miss, get yourself into bed. We'll sort things out in the morning."

"Yes, Mr. Smith."

I dragged myself across the dark yard, feeling suddenly so tired that my head spun. Major trotted beside me, but there was no sign of Patches. "Mathew?" I called softly into the night. There was no answer. I can't do anything about him now, I thought as I climbed wearily up the stairs to bed. Molly snored softly and didn't stir when I crawled in beside her. I felt tuckered out with excitement and worry. All night, strange dreams about barn fires, galloping horses, and lost children swirled through my sleep. Part of me didn't seem to sleep at all, just waited for morning so I could see that foal again. And so I could search for Mathew—and Patches too.

CHAPTER N.º 5

When Mrs. Smith called up the stairs, I could barely open my eyes. "Come on, Bo-Peep," said Molly. "You're slow as treacle."

I yawned, splashed cold water on my face from the wash jug, and fumbled into my clothes. I couldn't decide if what I felt most was excited to go and see the foal, scared to show my face in the kitchen because of being in trouble, or worried about Mathew. I wished I could stay in bed and go back to sleep. Slowly, I explained to Molly all that had happened the night before; she listened with wide eyes.

"Cor, you get into more trouble than me one and t'other, Bertie."

"Where is Bertie?" I asked.

Molly shrugged. "Dunno. Someplace workin' in a factory I s'pect. I ain't seen 'im for months."

When I walked into the kitchen, the family was already eating. Every face lifted from the plates of eggs and turned toward me.

"Well," Mrs. Smith said. "Why didn't you say the reason you went into the river?"

"How's our little farmer then?" asked Nathan teasingly.

"Fine," I answered. And then I announced, "I'm going to be an animal doctor."

The family gaped at me, then James chortled. "Ladies don't work in barns like that."

"Ladies can do anything they want to," I said. "My friend Edwina's sisters went to university, and one of them wants to be a lady doctor. So why can't there be lady veterinarians for horses?"

"Never mind university; just marry a farmer," said James. "Maybe Nathan will have

When I walked into the kitchen, the family was already eating. Every face lifted from the plates of eggs and turned toward me.

you. Can you cook? He's very partial to pancakes."

The boys elbowed each other in the ribs while my face flushed.

"Did Patches come home?" I asked, turning to Mr. Smith.

"No. Can't see any sign of that boy, either. We'll search after breakfast. Sit down to the table."

I forked my eggs in so fast that my tongue burned. I gulped anxiously, wondering wherever Mathew could be. And had he stolen my dog? He had no right to take Patches if he did! The eggs stuck in my throat, and my eyes stung.

"Right," said Mr. Smith when he finished the last of his breakfast. "Nathan, you take Prince to York Mills and see if you can find the boy. James, you search our fields. Molly and Millie, you search the barns and sheds."

"What will you do when you find him?" I asked. "You mustn't send him back!"

"We'll see," was all that Mr. Smith said, and he pulled his boots on. The rest of us followed him outside. All morning, after we'd fed the hens, Molly and I searched for Mathew. We looked under the buggy and the wagon in the drive shed, behind the cutter, in the loft. We searched the hay mow and the barn stalls. Briefly, I stopped to admire the mare and her foal; the new little horse's coat was dry and golden now. Its eyelashes curled. It had knobbly knees, and whiskers all around its soft mouth. I wanted to go into the stall and hug it but I didn't dare. Molly and I searched the musty root cellar and then walked all over the farm with James, calling Mathew's name. I called for Patches, too. I couldn't even think about the fact that I might never see his mischievous face again. He was *my* dog!

"Lummey, 'ow big is this bloomin' farm anyway?" Molly asked. "My feet 'urt."

"One hundred acres," said James. "My grand-father cut all the trees off it himself and pulled the stumps and hauled the rocks."

By lunch, no one had found either Patches or Mathew, and Mrs. Smith said we couldn't traipse around the countryside any more because there was so little time left until the wedding. Molly and I spent the afternoon polishing silver spoons and making bouquets of tulips and daffodils. Mrs. Smith went off with an axe to kill chickens for the wedding tea, and Molly and I had to sit on the porch and pluck the feathers. "This is disgusting," I muttered. The chickens' necks ended in bloody stumps. Their limp, warm bodies felt horrible on my knees. Feathers stuck to my fingers.

"Thought you wanted to doctor animals," Molly said. "Anyone can pluck hens."

I ignored her. My stomach rolled with worry. Tomorrow I had to go home—but how could I leave without Patches? And what would happen to Mathew? Tears slid down my cheeks without a sound and plopped onto the dead chicken on my lap.

When Mrs. Smith came to see how we were doing, she put her hand on my shoulder. "What's wrong, Millie?"

"Mathew is hungry and lost," I cried. "And Patches too—and I want to find them!"

"We'll look again later this evening. Now wash your hands at the pump and come to the barn. Don't you want to give that filly a name?" She smiled and gave my shoulder a rub, and I put down the dead hen. Molly came with us to the barn. The foal was asleep in the straw. I admired her fuzzy mane and smooth hindquarters, and thought about how I'd been there when she first came into the world. My face and Mathew's were the first human faces she ever saw. It was thrilling to think about this, and I didn't feel quite as badly right then about Mathew and Patches.

"Do you have a name?" asked Mrs. Smith.

"Honey," I replied, because the foal's coat was just the colour of the honey we spread on our toast each morning on the farm.

Mrs. Smith smiled again. "Next time you come to visit, she'll be running in the pasture. Now let's go and start on those apple pies."

The afternoon turned into evening, and the house and barn cast long shadows. The house smelled of daffodils as their buds opened in the wood stove's warmth. Our apple pies baked to golden sweetness; we had one for dessert, but the rest were saved for the wedding. The men went back out to the barn to milk the cows after dessert—they were late with their chores because of searching for Mathew. I kept listening for a scratch at the door, or for the sound of Mathew's voice calling my name from the darkness outside the porch. I knew this was a foolish wish, but I couldn't stop wishing it. It was like my wish that Father would walk in the door and say the war was over and he'd come home.

By bedtime I was too tired to wish any more. I simply crawled in beside Molly and fell asleep.

CHAPTER N.º 6

It was my last morning on the farm, and I managed to milk almost half a pail from Annabelle. Nathan teased me again and said that if I kept up the good work, maybe I'd be lucky enough to be married by a farmer. Everyone did their best to cheer me up and be kind. Mr. Smith said that Honey was a fine name for his new filly, and he let me into the stall so that I could groom the mare's legs and shoulders with a soft brush. I touched Honey's soft muzzle and fuzzy mane. In that moment I felt happy, but afterwards, packing my clothes into my little case, I felt like crying again. I wanted to touch Patches's wet nose, and stroke his brown spots.

"Pack this for your mother," Mrs. Smith said, coming into the room I had shared with Molly. She held out a packet wrapped in brown paper and tied with string. "There's a ham in there," she said, "from our own pigs. And I've got a dozen eggs downstairs for you. And some jam, and maple syrup from our woods, where you rode through the trilliums."

"Thank you, Mrs. Smith," I said. "Can I go and say goodbye to Prince?"

"He'll pull us to York Mills to the tram stop," she said. "Mrs Simcoe will meet us there."

Finally it was time to leave. Mr. Smith and Nathan and James were away working in the fields, and Molly was staying home to crochet lace edging for Amelia's pillowcases. She flung her arms around my neck and squeezed hard when we said goodbye. "Fink you can come again in the summer 'olidays?" she asked. "Or maybe I could come and visit you an' Edwina?"

"Yes," I agreed, although secretly I wondered whether I would be seeing Edwina again. It didn't seem as though we were going to be friends any more. "Or maybe we can go and visit my cousins on the lakes, and you can have a ride in my canoe."

"Cor, that would be grand! I'd give anyfink to do that! Can yer teach me to swim?"

"Yes, and to catch fish. Goodbye, Molly. I'll write you a letter."

"Ta, I'll write you back and tell yer about the wedding 'ighjinks! I'm going to stuff my face all afternoon!"

I laughed and climbed into the waiting buggy. Molly stood on the porch, with Major beside her, and waved as Prince trotted down the drive between the maple trees. I turned in my seat and waved back until Molly was just a speck, then a row of cedars blocked my view and I turned forward. I wished that Molly didn't have to live so far away, but at least she lived with a good family; she had good food to eat and clean clothes to wear, and a clean, plain room to sleep in. I remembered the slum she'd been living in when I first met her, and how dirty and sick her family had been. I was beginning to understand why my mother and Edwina's mother worked so hard at charity meetings to change conditions for women and children.

"What will happen to Mathew?" I asked in a small voice.

"Maybe he'll go back to Toronto and find the Dr. Barnardo home on Peter Street," Mrs Smith replied. "They'll send him to a farm where he's treated better. Or maybe he'll find work in the city. Or maybe he'll find work himself on another farm."

"As long a he doesn't have to be a tramp," I said.

Mrs. Smith drove with one hand and patted my shoulder with the other. "Let's hope he'll be fine," she said. "There are plenty of kind folk who'll help him if he gives them the chance. Just look how you rescued him from the Don River."

My cheeks glowed with pleasure.

Prince trotted steadily along the concession lines, between the spring fields where bluebirds sang and jays scolded. Dandelions bloomed in the ditches. When we reached York Mills, the bird-song was drowned out by the work in the mills and the rattle of buggy wheels and car motors on Yonge Street. Mrs. Smith tied Prince up outside the general store and I followed her in; she wanted to pick up her mail. I leaned against the counter, staring into the glass jars full of humbugs and mints.

"Millie, my dear child," said a familiar voice and I spun around to see my mother smiling at me.

"Mother!" I flung myself into her arms; it felt as though I hadn't seen her for weeks. "But where's Mrs. Simcoe?"

"I decided to come and fetch you home myself, and to thank Mrs. Smith for having you to stay."

"It's been a pleasure," Mrs Smith said, with her hands full of envelopes. I waited breathlessly to see if she'd tell Mother about all the trouble I'd got into with nearly drowning and being in the barn late at night, but she all she said was, "Your daughter's a good worker. We've had so much to do on account of this spring wedding."

"I'm happy she could assist you," Mother replied graciously. "Now, I believe it's time for the radial to take us home."

"I'll fetch her case from the buggy," Mrs Smith said, and swung the door open. Outside the general store was something white—something white and small with brown spots.

"Patches!" I screamed, and he stopped digging in the dirt and rushed to me and leapt into my arms. I almost fell over backwards. "Oh, Patches, where have you been?" I buried my face in his coat and felt his tongue lick my cheeks.

"Whatever is going on?" asked Mother.

"He's mine, can I keep him? Oh, Mother, he's a stray and I don't want him to be like a beggar. He ran away from the farm and now I've found him again and please can we take him home, Mother?"

Behind me, I heard the radial approaching, its brakes squealing. Passengers jostled on the wooden sidewalk, and Mrs. Smith waited to hand over my case and a basket of produce she was sending with me.

"Mercy!" said Mother.

"Please!" I cried. "Please, Mother?"

"He's a good dog—you'll never worry about rats again," said Mrs. Smith.

Mother's mouth twitched at the corners. "Oh, Millie, you harum-scarum," she said. "Climb on board and bring Patches home."

"Yes!"

I scrambled up the steps, clutching Patches, and fell into the closest seat. Mother sat beside me just as the tram began to move again, gathering speed. I waved out the window until Mrs. Smith and Prince were lost to view. Patches licked Mother's gloved hands, and she laughed. "The lost is found," she said. "And that reminds me, Millie." She slid a hand into her coat pocket and took out my mouth organ. I gaped. "Edwina brought this to the house yesterday and said to tell you she's very sorry it was ever lost. She's coming for tea when we get home this evening."

I gripped the mouth organ in my own hand, and let myself be jolted back toward the city, smiling all the way. Wait until Edwina sees Patches, I thought. Maybe we can buy him a red leather collar!

GLOSSARY OF COCKNEY RHYMING SLANG

Bath buns: sons

Botany Bay: run away

cut and carried: married

Gates of Rome: home

one and t'other: brother

BIBLIOGRAPHY

TEXT

Berchem, F. R. *Opportunity Road: Yonge Street 1860–1939*. Toronto: Natural Heritage, 1996.

Careless, J.M.S. *Toronto to 1918: An Illustrated History*. Toronto: James Lorimer, 1984.

Corbett, Gail H. *Nation Builders: Barnardo Children in Canada*. Toronto: Dundurn, 1997.

Hall, Roger, and Gordon Dodds. *Ontario: Two Hundred Years in Pictures*. Toronto: Dundurn, 1991.

Hart, Patricia W. *Pioneering in North York: A History of the Borough*. Toronto: General Publishing, 1968.

Hoffman, Frances, and Ryan Taylor. *Much to Be Done: Private Life in Ontario from Victorian Diaries*. Toronto: Natural Heritage, 1996.

Ladell, James, and Monica Ladell. *A Farm in the Family: The Many Faces of Ontario Agriculture over the Centuries*. Toronto: Dundurn, 1985.

WEB

The Fund the Child Movement. "A Timeline of Caregiving Labor." http://fundthechild.tripod.com/id2.html, n.d.

Windsor Occupational Health Information Services. "A History of the Occupational Health and Safety Act." http://www.wohis.org/history.htm, n.d.

Dear Reader,

This has been the fourth and final book about Millie. We hope you've enjoyed meeting and getting to know her as much as we have enjoyed bringing her—and her wonderful story—to you.

Although Millie's tale is told, there are still eleven more terrific girls to read about, whose exciting adventures take place in Canada's past—girls just like you. So do keep on reading!

And please—don't forget to keep in touch! We love receiving your incredible letters telling us about your favourite stories and which girls you like best. And thank you for telling us about the stories you would like to read! There are so many remarkable stories in Canadian history. It seems that wherever we live, great stories live too, in our towns and cities, on our rivers and mountains. We hope that Our Canadian Girl *captures the richness of that past.*

Sincerely,
Barbara Berson
Editor

1608
Samuel de Champlain establishes the first fortified trading post at Quebec.

1759
The British defeat the French in the Battle of the Plains of Abraham.

1812
The United States declares war against Canada.

1845
The expedition of Sir John Franklin to the Arctic ends when the ship is frozen in the pack ice; the fate of its crew remains a mystery.

1869
Louis Riel leads his Metis followers in the Red River Rebellion.

18
Brit Colu joi Can

1755
The British expel the entire French population of Acadia (today's Maritime provinces), sending them into exile.

1776
The 13 Colonies revolt against Britain, and the Loyalists flee to Canada.

1837
Calling for responsible government, the Patriotes, following Louis-Joseph Papineau, rebel in Lower Canada; William Lyon Mackenzie leads the uprising in Upper Canada.

1867
New Brunswick, Nova Scotia, and the United Province of Canada come together in Confederation to form the Dominion of Canada.

1870
Manitoba jo Canada. T Northwes Territorie become an official territory o Canada.

1784
Rachel

Timeline

1885
At Craigellachie, British Columbia, the last spike is driven to complete the building of the Canadian Pacific Railway.

1898
The Yukon Territory becomes an official territory of Canada.

1914
Britain declares war on Germany, and Canada, because of its ties to Britain, is at war too.

1918
As a result of the Wartime Elections Act, the women of Canada are given the right to vote in federal elections.

1945
World War II ends conclusively with the dropping of atomic bombs on Hiroshima and Nagasaki.

1873
Prince Edward Island joins Canada.

1896
Gold is discovered on Bonanza Creek, a tributary of the Klondike River.

1905
Alberta and Saskatchewan join Canada.

1917
In the Halifax harbour, two ships collide, causing an explosion that leaves more than 1,600 dead and 9,000 injured.

1939
Canada declares war on Germany seven days after war is declared by Britain and France.

1949
Newfoundland, under the leadership of Joey Smallwood, joins Canada.

1903
Keeley

1885
Marie-Claire

1915
Millie